TWO SHORTS
AND
A
SNORT

JAN SIKES

ISBN: 0-9906179-9-8
ISBN-13: 978-0-9906179-9-0

Obsessed was inspired by a song, "Lights of Loving County," written by Charlie Robison and Jack Ingram.

JAN SIKES

CONTENTS

OBSESSED

1964 found the oil business booming out in far West Texas. Rigs stretched as far as the eye could see and at night they sparkled against the black sky like thousands of diamonds. It was a time when a man could quit a job on one rig, go down the road and have a new one making ten cents per hour more before the end of the day. It created a new breed of men — the roughnecks. But, it wasn't the rigs that drove a man crazy sometimes. No, sometimes it was a need that ran deeper than the roots of the Mesquite trees. It could be aptly called obsession.

Charlie Riddle jumped out of the pickup truck almost before it came to a stop in front of The Dew Drop Inn. A neon sign blinked off and on, and snow flurries changed colors as they drifted in front of it.

"What's your hurry, Charlie?" Robert called.

"Shit, man. I'm ready for a beer. I've got a week's pay and a hunnert dollars of coke in my pocket. It's time to party." Charlie pushed through the door.

He stopped short three steps inside, then strode to the back of the bar. "Nelda Sue! What in the hell are you doing here?" He put his hands on the table and stared at the man seated across from her. "And with this damn oil bum?"

"Charlie Riddle, I have you know I am a grown woman. I can go anywhere I want with anyone I want." Nelda Sue tossed her head. "Besides, until a ring is on my finger, you or no one else owns me."

The man got to his feet. "You better just move on along, Charlie. I don't want no trouble."

Charlie stood toe-to-toe with him. The men matched each other in height at six-foot-two, but the similarities ended there. Blonde, tanned, and muscled, Charlie outweighed dark-haired Pete by fifty pounds.

"Just because your daddy owns the oil company, Petey boy, don't mean you get to tell me what to do, you sonofabitch." Charlie spit on the floor.

Nelda Sue pushed away from the table, reached for her mouton fur coat and took the man's hand. "Let's go somewhere else, Pete. There's more than one bar in this town."

Charlie grabbed her arm. "Come on, Nelda Sue. You don't really want to be with this guy, and you know it. Come party with me. I'm off for forty-eight hours. You know we always have a real good time."

Pete shoved Charlie. "Get your hands off her, Riddle."

Charlie pushed him backward against the table and sent beer bottles flying.

The bouncer, along with Charlie's friend, got to them before the men exchanged blows.

"Let it go, Charlie," Robert said. "She ain't worth it. Let's get a beer."

Nelda Sue tossed her red hair, tugged on her mini-skirt that almost covered black lace panties, and turned toward Pete. "Let's go."

The two hurried to the door.

Charlie yelled, "I'm gonna marry you, Nelda Sue! Do you hear me? I said I'm gonna marry you."

Nelda strutted back to him. "Like I told you, Charlie, until there is a ring on my hand no one gets to tell me what to do." She waved her left hand in front of his face. "Do you see a ring? Huh? Do you?"

Charlie didn't answer.

"That's what I thought." She rushed back to Pete, and they pushed through the door and out into the night.

Robert slapped Charlie on the back. "Come on, man. Let's get some beers."

Charlie joined Robert at the bar, but he was mad. Dammit! He thought he had an agreement with Nelda Sue. He'd even paid her damn rent on the trailer in Monahans last month. He worked overtime on the rig, so he could buy her nice things. Surely that counted for something. And, she was damned good in the sack.

He chugged his first beer and slammed the bottle down. "Give me something stronger, barkeep."

"Hey, Charlie, look who just came in the door." Robert nudged his friend and pointed. "Ain't that the two gals that came out to the rig last week?"

Charlie squinted. "Maybe," he said sullenly.

"Well, if it is, we can get some guaranteed pussy."

"Ain't interested," Charlie replied.

"Shit, you've got it bad for Nelda Sue. I think you better either forget her or marry her one or the other."

Charlie shrugged and pounded on the bar. "Come on, man. A shot of whiskey. Make it a double."

All he could think about was Nelda Sue's satin skin, luscious lips, and the sway of her rounded hips under that mini-skirt. And, the fact that she was out with that oil company bum burned a hole in his gut.

After a while, Robert stood up. "You can sit here and brood all you want, but I'm gonna go find some action. Hell, it's our days off. Enjoy 'em. We've earned some fun."

Charlie stared into the empty shot glass. "Go on, man. I've got some thinkin' to do."

Robert headed toward a table where the two women sat.

Charlie swiveled on the barstool to get a better look. Hell, he ought to go on over there with him. The brunette wasn't bad looking. But, all he could think about was Nelda Sue.

He got to his feet and escaped to the men's room. Inside a stall, he pulled out a plastic bag from his jean pocket, rolled up a dollar bill and made two straight lines of white powder on the back side of his wallet.

A shiver ran through him as the powder went up his nose. He wet his finger, wiped the residue off the wallet and stuck it along with the plastic bag back in his pocket.

He relieved himself and gave a quick glance in the mirror to make

sure no white powder remnants could be seen. With resolve, he strode back into the bar to find his friend.

"Hey, man, I've gotta get out of here. You ready to go?"

Robert narrowed his eyes. "Hell no, I'm not ready to go. I haven't even told my best jokes to these girls yet."

"Well, I'm leavin'. Either come with me or find another ride home."

"Shit, man, I'm stayin'. And, if you get your ass thrown in jail tonight, don't call me for bail money."

The brunette put her arm around Robert's waist. "Don't worry, hon, me and Lola can take you home. Stay here and party with us."

Robert grinned. "That's damned hospitable, sweetheart. Charlie, go on, but you stay out of trouble. You hear?"

Charlie waved over his shoulder as he made for the door.

He cranked up the pickup and turned the heater on full blast. It took a few minutes for the snowflakes to melt enough to see the road. He was high, and a little drunk and the frozen droplets sparkled like a thousand tiny diamonds in the lights.

When he could see, he threw the truck in reverse and drove. *They had to be at another bar.* He covered the strip on the Andrews Highway without seeing the Standard Oil pickup he knew Pete always drove.

He slammed his fist into the dash. He had to figure out something. He had to put a ring on Nelda Sue's finger.

After checking the dives on the other side of town, he pulled into the parking lot of The New Rainbow Bar.

He snorted more Coke before he went in. His head buzzed, and he needed a stiff drink. With a whiskey and seven in hand, he sat at the bar hunched over hoping it would discourage any conversation. Thankfully, the jukebox in the corner blared, drowning out everything but his thoughts.

Halfway into his fifth drink, the door flew open and in walked a woman looking richer than sin. With an expensive fur around her shoulders, and ten years' worth of work on her hand, she caught his eye.

Why would a rich woman be out alone and in a seedy bar?

Without taking his eyes off her, he continued to drink. An idea formed in his messed-up mind. That diamond on her left hand was the solution to all his problems with Nelda Sue.

He figured she was there to meet up with a lover. And even though she never took her eyes off the door, no one came.

After she'd downed two drinks, she pulled her fur around her shoulders and stomped out into the night.

Charlie threw money on the bar and followed.

What happened after that became a blur. Charlie remembered parking outside her house and waiting for hours to make sure she was alone. Vaguely he recalled putting his gun to her head. He hadn't intended to pull the trigger, but she started to scream.

Then, he jerked the diamond ring off her hand and left her lying in a pool of blood. He tossed the gun into the shrubbery, jumped into his pickup and roared off.

Now, Nelda Sue would be his!

Driving well over the speed limit, it didn't take him long to reach Monahans. It was four in the morning when he came to a stop in front of Nelda Sue's trailer. No lights shone in the windows. What if she wasn't home? He pounded on the door. "Open up, Nelda Sue. It's me, Charlie."

She didn't answer. He pounded harder. A dog barked down the street and lights appeared in a neighboring trailer.

"Damn!" Charlie cursed. *She was still out with that sonofabitch. She probably wouldn't be home until morning.*

Glad he had a six pack of beer in the truck, he pulled around the corner out of sight to wait.

Sure enough, as the sun peeked over the horizon, the familiar pickup with the Standard Oil logo on the side came to a stop in front of the trailer.

Charlie ground his teeth as he watched Nelda Sue kiss Pete, before she jumped out and ran up to her front door.

Wasting no time, Charlie pulled back around as soon as the pickup was out of sight.

He pounded on the door. "Open up, Nelda Sue. It's me, Charlie. I have something for you."

Nelda Sue opened the door. "I swear, Charlie Riddle. You are persistent."

Charlie grinned. "Hi, sugar. Aren't you gonna invite me in?"

She stood aside. "Come on in."

As soon as she closed the door, Charlie knelt on one knee. "Nelda Sue, will you marry me?"

"Oh, Charlie. Get up, will you? We both know you don't have a ring to put on my finger."

Charlie opened his hand. The stolen diamond ring sparkled. "You might want to think again, sweetheart."

She reached for the ring and gasped. "It's beautiful." She narrowed her eyes. "Where did you get this?"

"I bought it. I love you, Nelda Sue, and I want you to be mine." He stood and brought her into his arms. "Please say yes."

The ring slid onto her finger, and she held it up so that the light glinted off it. She grinned. "Yes, Charlie Riddle. I'll marry you."

Charlie let out a whoop and picked her up. He kissed her with a forceful hunger while he carried her to the bedroom.

They spent the rest of the day and that night together. They snorted the remainder of Charlie's Cocaine and went to the liquor store for more booze.

The next morning, Charlie sat across the table from his future wife with a steaming cup of coffee. "Now, you remember what I told you, Nelda Sue?"

"Yes, I remember. I can't tell anyone yet about the ring or show it to anyone. Not for two more weeks."

"Yep. That's it. Then we'll leave, me and you. I can work the rigs out in South Alabama, and we'll start a whole new life there."

Charlie kissed her long and deep before he left to go to work. "I'll see you soon. You start gettin' packed up to move. I'll be back for you with money in my pocket."

TWO SHORTS AND A SNORT

She stood in the door and waved as he pulled out on the road.

Two days later, Robert came to work and slapped Charlie on the back. "Hell, man. I didn't think you'd do it."

"Do what?"

"Put a ring on Nelda Sue's hand."

"How do you know?"

"Shit! She's sashaying all around town showing everyone and telling them you and her are gettin' hitched. Congratulations!"

Charlie threw down the wrench he had in his hand and ran to his truck.

"Hey! Where are you going?" Robert yelled.

Gravel spun under the tires when Charlie took off. He ran his hand through his hair and ground his teeth. What to do?

He pointed his pickup toward Mexico. If he could get across the border, they couldn't touch him, and he could send for Nelda Sue.

A roadside rest area sign caught his eye, so he pulled in. He had to think.

After a few minutes, he rummaged through his glove box looking for any pills or cocaine he might have left there. His fingers found a tin box shoved way in the back.

He opened it and dumped the powder onto a picnic table. Then, he snorted it until every tiny particle disappeared. Eyes wide and his heart beating fast, he got back on the road.

But something inside Charlie Riddle snapped. Thoughts didn't connect. The white lines on the road taunted and teased him.

He made it to El Paso before his truck ran out of gas and his mind couldn't make a sensible thought. Without looking back, he abandoned the pickup on the side of the road.

For two days and nights, he wandered the streets aimlessly until a policeman finally picked him up for vagrancy.

***

It didn't take long for law enforcement to connect the dots. They buried that sheriff's poor wife with the diamond ring he'd stolen on her hand.

TWO SHORTS AND A SNORT

A life sentence in Huntsville prison for pre-meditated murder was all his obsession cost him.

***

Charlie sat hunched over in his cell and opened a letter from Robert. He read it, crumpled the paper and tossed into a trash can. He knew Nelda Sue had married Pete, and now she's given birth to his son.

Charlie dropped his head into his hands and wept.

THE END

Moral of the story: When the price tag is too high, walk away.

JAN SIKES

MAGGIE

Jackson Durant tugged at the brim of his hat and pulled his collar up around his ears. "Damn longhorn," he muttered.

He turned his roan to the South putting the bitter North wind at his back. Thick snow prevented visibility much farther than a hand in front of his face. Tracks he'd been following disappeared under the white layer.

Might as well head on back. He wasn't going to find the ornery critter in this storm.

His ears perked up. "Whoa, boy."

He sat still. There it was again. Damned if it didn't sound like a baby crying. He turned his horse toward the sound.

"What the hell?" He slid from the saddle at an outcropping of rocks.

A small basket sat under a ledge out of the snow. Jackson knelt beside it and pulled back a blanket. The bluest eyes he'd ever seen stared up at him. A note tucked inside the blanket fluttered in the wind. He jerked his gloves off and fumbled to open it with cold, stiff fingers. *I'm so sorry. Please take care of my baby.*

His heart lurched. He jumped to his feet and turned in a full circle. "Hello. Hello. Is anyone out there?"

No answer, except for the wind.

One thing for certain, the infant wouldn't last long in this storm. A million questions swarmed around his head like angry bees.

He'd sort it all out later. For now, he had to get the baby to safety. He lifted the basket onto the roan and tied it securely around the saddle horn, then swung his long legs up and turned toward home.

Mary greeted him at the door. "Oh Jax, I've been so worried…" She stopped in mid-sentence.

"What?"

"I don't know, honey. I found this basket under an outcropping in the south pasture." He passed her the note.

She unfolded it with trembling fingers, then gazed up with tears shimmering in her eyes. "I want to hold him."

Jackson sat the basket on a table and Mary unwrapped the layers of blankets. The baby gurgled and kicked its feet.

She lifted the child and clutched it to her bosom. "I'm afraid I prayed this baby up, Jax."

He draped an arm across her shoulders. "Now, honey, you didn't conjure up this child. Some desperate mother needed help. As soon as this storm lets up, I'll try and get some answers. I do know the basket hadn't been there long because it was still warm when I found it."

"I'll bet he's hungry." Mary sank into a rocker. "Can you find me a new rubber glove? I think I can create a makeshift bottle."

Jackson shucked his coat, gloves, and hat and rummaged through the pantry. His heart pounded in his chest. Could he be asleep and dreaming? He walked back into the living room.

Mary looked up with a wide smile when he returned. "It's a girl, Jax. A girl."

He knelt beside the chair. His heart melted when the baby wrapped her tiny hand around his little finger. "She's beautiful and perfect, Mary. But, she has a mother somewhere, and I'll find her. She must be in a desperate situation to have left her sweet baby like that."

Mary nodded. "Will you hold her while I rig up a bottle? As soon as this storm lets up, we need to go into town and get some proper things for her."

Jackson took the child and gazed at her pink face, marveling at how tiny she felt in his large hands. It was all surreal. He and Mary had tried for over five years to conceive a child, and he knew the longing only too well. Maybe God had answered their prayers.

"Magdalene," he said.

"What?" Mary called from the kitchen.

"Let's name her Magdalene, and we can call her Maggie."

"That is if we can't find her mother." Mary reached for the baby.

Mary and Jackson laughed out loud when the baby sucked noisily on the tip of the rubber glove.

* * *

TWO SHORTS AND A SNORT

Neither Jackson nor Mary Durant slept much that night. The next morning after breakfast, he saddled the roan and rode back to the south pasture. He still had a longhorn to find, but more than that, answers.

He kept his eye to the ground searching for tracks…any kind of tracks — human or bovine.

When he reached the outcropping, he raised binoculars and scanned the area. A piece of red fabric in a snowdrift caught his eye.

Wasting no time, he dismounted and hurried to the drift.

He brushed the snow away to find sightless eyes and a battered face staring up at him. He worked to get the stiff body out and tied the woman across the rump of the roan. At least, she deserved a decent burial. And, he'd report it to the sheriff as soon as he could get into town.

Just as he swung up into the saddle, the distinct bellowing of a longhorn reached his ears. He turned to see the ornery elusive bovine lumbering toward him.

"You beat all I ever saw," he yelled as he turned the horse toward home and clicked his tongue.

He swiveled in the saddle to see the animal following him.

Could it be that the Angels used the longhorn to lure him out into the storm?

Whatever the causes or reasons, Jackson and Mary Durant now had a beautiful baby girl, Maggie.

THE END

Moral of the story: Be careful what you wish for; you just might get it.

FRIENDS INSTEAD OF LOVERS

I won't forget the day we met
We hit it off just right
I felt like I had known you
Dang near all my life
As time went by we grew so close
We shared our ups and downs
Then one night, we crossed the
line

We laid a blanket on the ground
But, I think I liked you better
When we were friends instead of
lovers

Now in secret rendezvous
We meet, and we make love
Our passions rise so high and
free
It's all we're thinking of
I love the way we make love
Baby, I won't lie
But when I see you in daylight
You won't look me in the eye
I think I liked you better
The way it was before

The way we shared our hopes, our dreams,

Our fears and so much more

Yes, I think I liked you better

When we were friends instead of lovers

Yep, I know I liked you better

When we were friends instead of lovers

THE END

A WORD FROM THE AUTHOR

I sincerely hope you have enjoyed these vignettes. I wrote them as a response to the 90-day Alpha/Omega Beginning To End Short Story challenge issued by THE RAVE REVIEWS BOOK CLUB.

If you've enjoyed these stories, I hope you will be so kind as to leave a review and check out my other books.

FLOWERS AND STONE

THE CONVICT AND THE ROSE

HOME AT LAST

'TIL DEATH DO US PART

DISCOVERY - POETRY AND ART

ABOUT THE AUTHOR

Multi-Award-winning author, Jan Sikes, weaves stories in a creative and entertaining way. She has been called a magician and wordsmith extraordinaire by her readers and peers.

Jan published a series of four biographical fiction books about a Texas musician who was a pioneer in the Outlaw Music movement before it ever had a name. Along with each book, she released a corresponding music CD of original songs. And, she's also published a beautiful poetry and art book and five short stories. Her current project is a series of paranormal romance novels.

Jan plays guitar, writes songs, poetry, short stories, screenplays and novels. She resides in North Texas, serves on the **RWISA (RAVE WRITERS INT'L SOCIETY OF AUTHORS)** Executive Committee and hosts a radio show, "Aspire to Inspire" for the **RAVE REVIEWS BOOK CLUB.** She serves actively in Texas organizations dedicated to preserving and promoting literacy. Employed as a staff writer for an Oklahoma magazine and BUDDY Magazine (The Original Texas Music Magazine), Jan keeps her finger on the music pulse of Texas. In her spare time, she volunteers at music festivals and supports local authors and artists.

JAN'S WEBSITE: http://www.jansikes.com

BLOG: http://www.rijanjks.wordpress.com

TWITTER:
http://www.twitter.com/rijanjks

FACEBOOK:
http://www.facebook.com/authorjansikesbooks

AMAZON AUTHOR CENTRAL:
https://www.amazon.com/Jan-Sikes/e/B00CS9K8DK/

JAN SIKES

RiJan Publishing

Chapter 1

Darlina Flowers adjusted her silver midriff top and black satin shorts while she stood at the counter waiting for the next food order. Her gaze wandered around the dimly lit nightclub. Plumes of smoke swirled around the large mirrored ball hanging from the ceiling, as electric yellow, red, blue and green reflected on the ceiling. The sights and sounds of the club had become familiar and comfortable. A vision of her strict religious mother frowning at her flashed through her mind for a brief second. Her mother never hesitated to express her disappointment with Darlina's chosen lifestyle.

The band began a boisterous performance of *Proud Mary*, and she unconsciously moved to the beat of the drum. She often pondered why the places and things forbidden by the church and her mother drew her the most.

Her musings were interrupted by her boss. Marketa had not been in America long enough to lose her thick Czechoslovakian accent. "Darlina, when it's your turn, I want you to try those moves.

The customers love it."

"I'll try, but I'm not sure I can." She focused her attention on the stage and how her friend, Sherry, shook her hips and shimmied her boobs at the same time to the rhythm of the music.

Darlina truly enjoyed the time she spent at the nightclub. When Marketa had approached her about working for tips and learning to dance, she never imagined she would have the confidence to be in the spotlight.

"You're up." Marketa affectionately patted her arm. "Show me how it's done."

Darlina climbed the steps to the stage amidst whistles and catcalls. Her insides churned as if hundreds of butterflies fluttered around. She turned to the band leader, a burly man everyone called Buffalo. "Let's do *Suzie Q*."

He took a noisy slurp from his drink. "Okay, little lady."

While the band played, she moved her hips concentrating on the beat of the music. Within seconds, the nerves settled, and her movements became more fluid.

"Keep it sexy but clean," Marketa taught her.

That wasn't hard for her since she knew

very little about "dirty."

Just as her dance performance came to an end, a commotion drew her attention. Turning, she saw Marketa personally escorting a group of customers to the best table in the club. It was totally out of character for this spitfire of a woman to make a fuss over anyone. Marketa flitted around with her long elegant ivory cigarette holder in her hand.

Amidst enthusiastic applause, the bright spotlight now off her, Darlina hurried to talk to Sherry.

"Who is that?"

Sherry rolled her eyes. "That's Luke Stone and the Rebel Rousers. I can't believe you don't know that."

"How would I know? You forget I don't get out much other than here."

"They are only the hottest band in the whole State of Texas."

"Do you know them?"

"Hell yes, I know 'em. Had a one-night stand with the drummer a year or so ago."

With overwhelming curiosity, Darlina proposed, "Let me wait their table."

Sherry shrugged her shoulders, "Suits me."

Darlina hurried to the table carrying menus. "Evening folks, I'm Darlina, and I'll be taking care of you tonight."

Luke Stone, an assuming man over six feet tall with a swagger and crooked grin promptly replied, "Honey, are you sure about that?"

A hot flush spread across her cheeks at his implication. "Let me re-phrase that. I'll be taking your order tonight. What can I get you to drink?"

"Well, seein' as how you don't serve whiskey here, guess I'll be havin' a cup of coffee," Luke said, leaning back in his chair and lighting a King Edward cigar.

Darlina worked her way around the table taking everyone's drink orders. Luke's stare bore a hole through her, and it made her more than a little uncomfortable.

Rushing to the counter to fill the orders, she heard Buffalo's voice boom from the stage. "Folks, we are real honored to have Luke Stone and the Rebel Rousers in here tonight. I wanna dedicate this next song to them." The band played a rousing rendition of *The Fightin' Side of Me*.

Luke yelled from his table, "Hell Yeah!"

Darlina stood where she could watch this

group. It appeared that Luke Stone was the man in charge and everyone around him either seemed to respect and love him or fear him. She couldn't tell which, and maybe it was a little of both.

The attractive dark-haired lady to the left of him must be his wife, she concluded. Many of the customers approached his table, and he seemed to know them all personally.

Sherry joined her. "Whatcha' lookin' at, sweetie?"

She quickly looked away. "Just watchin' the show."

"Let me give you a little advice. Luke Stone is bad news. And besides that, he's way too old for you."

"I have no intention of getting any closer to him than to take his order and serve his food."

She knew in her heart the words that came out of her mouth weren't true. He fascinated her. It's just curiosity, she told herself. She also figured he'd never give her the time of day.

Marketa continued to hover around Luke's table while Darlina served drinks to the group. "Luke, this is Darlina, my up and coming new dancing star and I'm anxious for you to see her perform."

Luke flashed his crooked grin. "Marketa, everyone knows you've got the best dancin' girls in Abilene. I'll look forward to it."

Darlina blushed at the compliment. "Is everyone ready to order?"

She avoided eye contact with Luke while he placed his order. She didn't know why this man unnerved her so, but it seemed as if he could see straight through her. She retreated to the safety of the counter to wait for their food.

Marketa sought her out. "Honey, I want you to take another turn up on the stage, so Luke can see you dance."

Darlina almost choked on her Coke, and replied somewhat breathlessly, "Oh Marketa, I feel really nervous all of a sudden."

Marketa threw back her bleached blonde head and laughed. "Luke Stone has that effect on women. Don't worry; he'll love you."

"I think that's what I'm afraid of," Darlina muttered.

As she climbed the steps to the stage, Luke's distinctive voice rang out. "Alright! Now we're gonna get some entertainment."

Darlina called to Buffalo, "Play *Mustang Sally.*"

The music started, and she tried to forget about a certain pair of eyes out in the audience. After a few seconds into the song, she relaxed and danced, remembering every move Marketa had taught her.

She finished to whoops and hollers from all over the club.

Marketa rushed up to meet her as she came off the stage. "That was perfect! I knew you could do it!"

Passing through the crowd, everyone showered Darlina with compliments for the performance. Breathless and exhilarated, she reached the counter to gather Luke Stone's order, suddenly no longer shy about approaching him.

She'd performed well, and it gave her confidence. Smiling directly at Luke, she placed the food in front of him.

He put his arm around her waist. "Little lady, you did a hell of a job up there. I really enjoyed watchin' you." He winked as if to emphasize some hidden meaning.

Darlina placed her hand lightly on Luke's shoulder. "Thank you so much. I'm really glad you enjoyed it."

As she started to move away, he asked. "Where are you runnin' off to so fast?"

"Gotta get the rest of these orders out."

"Come back and talk to me."

"Sure, soon as I get a minute," she said over her shoulder as she hurried off, pleased that Luke wanted to talk to her.

She continued bringing the rest of the food to the table and then moved back to the counter after flashing Luke another warm smile.

"What in the hell do you think you're doing?" Sherry did not try to hide her agitation.

"I'm just doin' my job."

"You're flirting with Luke Stone."

Darlina twisted a lock of hair around her finger. "No I'm not. I'm bein' friendly 'cause I want a good tip."

"I wasn't born yesterday, honey. I know what I see. I also know Luke. With your blue eyes and long auburn hair, he's gonna be after you like a duck after a June bug."

Darlina brushed her friend's accusation aside, but her pulse quickened when she looked toward Luke and his group.

An hour later, she collected the empty dishes. "Can I get y'all anything else?"

Luke motioned, "Down here, honey."

She walked to the end of the table where he sat.

"Sugar, I'd like to invite you to go to the motel with me and Mary tonight."

Shaking her head, she replied. "I have no idea what you're asking me, but the answer is no."

"Come on," Luke insisted. "We'll make sure you have a real good time."

Darlina cast a glance at the woman she assumed was Mary only to see her smiling openly at her. "I appreciate the invite, Mr. Stone, but the answer is still no."

"Oh, come on now, and don't call me Mr. Stone. I'm Luke, and this here is Mary. I promise you we can have one hell of a good time." Luke stood and put his arm around Darlina's waist.

His warm hand on her bare skin made her heart race, and she pulled away. "Luke, it's been great meeting you tonight, but I truly don't know what you're talking about and I've gotta go. Y'all come in and see us again."

Luke released her smiling. "Sugar, you can bet on that!"

The rest of the group joined him, and they left the club. He looked back when he reached the door, winked at Darlina, and then held the door for Mary as they disappeared into the night.

A confused and shaken Darlina quickly gathered the rest of the dishes from the table, finding a sizable tip.

Sherry was once again waiting for her when she returned with the dishes. "Honey, you're playing with fire if you have anything to do with him."

"He wanted me to go with him and his lady to a motel. I don't know much, but that sure seems wrong. I don't understand why he would ask me that and especially right in front of her."

"You have lots to learn, Darlina. He wanted to have a three-way." Sherry laughed out loud.

"All three of us at the same time?"

"Yes, sweetie, at the same time."

Her face flushed with embarrassment. "Well, I guess that certainly is different."

"Different is one way to describe Luke Stone."

On her way home that night, Darlina couldn't stop thinking about Luke Stone, his handsome face, the arrogance, his crooked grin and the indecent proposal. She knew she wanted to see him again.

I hope you've enjoyed this peek into "Flowers and Stone."

www.ingramcontent.com/pod-product-compliance
Lightning Source LLC
Chambersburg PA
CBHW020606130626
46552CB00007B/3069